Molly Mischief

My Best Job

GROSSET & DUNLAP
An Imprint of Penguin Random House LLC, New York

Penguin supports copyright. Copyright fuels creativity, encourages diverse voices,
promotes free speech, and creates a vibrant culture. Thank you for buying an authorized
edition of this book and for complying with copyright laws by not reproducing, scanning,
or distributing any part of it in any form without permission. You are supporting writers
and allowing Penguin to continue to publish books for every reader.

Copyright © 2018 by Adam Hargreaves. All rights reserved.
First published as *Molly Mischief: When I Grow Up* in the United Kingdom in 2018 by Pavilion Books Limited.
First published in the United States in 2019 by Grosset & Dunlap,
an imprint of Penguin Random House LLC, New York.
GROSSET & DUNLAP is a trademark of Penguin Random House LLC. Manufactured in China.

Visit us at www.penguinrandomhouse.com.

Library of Congress Cataloging-in-Publication Data is available upon request.

ISBN 9781524788063   10 9 8 7 6 5 4 3 2 1

Molly Mischief

My Best Job

Adam Hargreaves

Grosset & Dunlap

Hello, my name is **Molly**.

Some people call me **Molly Mischief**—
I have no idea why!

My mom and dad are always telling me what to do.

It's always **time** to do something.

Time for school.

MOLLY!

And time to go to bed. Way too early!

MOLLY!

I can't wait until I grow up.
Then Mom and Dad won't
be able to tell me what to do.

When I grow up, I'll be able to do anything I like.
I'll even get a job.

Maybe when I grow up, I'll be an **astronaut.**

Then again, maybe being an astronaut is not such a good idea.

I know—I'll be a firefighter.

That would be fun . . .

I'd bake the best cakes in
the world.

I could be a scientist . . .

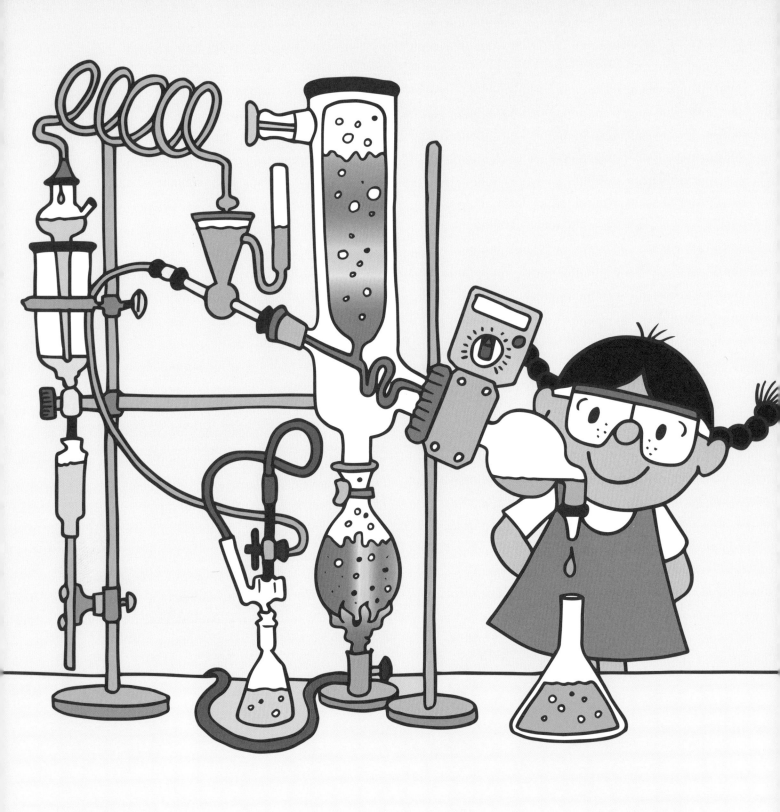

. . . and invent an amazing new invention.

BANG!

Maybe not.

Or a pop star!

MOLLY!

Maybe a deep-sea diver?

I'm good at making people laugh.

Except for Dad!

MOLLY!

I really like reading.
Being a librarian would be perfect.

But I'm definitely too loud
for that job.

Then I had a thought.
Having a job meant that I wouldn't have time to play with my friends.

I wouldn't have time
to build tree houses.

I wouldn't have time to paint pictures.

I wouldn't even have time to tease my brother!

Do you know what?
I don't want to grow up.
Not yet, anyway.

**Maybe Mom and Dad are right,
because to do all the things I want to when I grow up,
I'll need to be smart and healthy.**

. . . is being me!

SPLAT!